THE BROONS
and
OOR WULLIE
1939-1945
THE LIGHTER SIDE OF WORLD WAR II

Adapted from the frontispiece of the 1941 Broons Book.

WATTY

ISBN 0-85116-651-2
Printed and published in Great Britain by D.C. Thomson & Co., Ltd., 185 Fleet Street, London EC4A 2HS. © D.C. Thomson & Co., Ltd., 1997.

1939

As soon as war was declared on September 3rd, plans were put into action to call up men to the Armed Forces, and arrangements made to evacuate over two million mothers and children from major cities to outlying areas. In Scotland, 190,000 were evacuated from Glasgow alone, while many from Edinburgh were sent to St. Andrews. Kirriemuir and Brechin were amongst those towns to take in children from Dundee.
Even Scotland's famous spiky-haired laddie, Oor Wullie, found himself in the countryside...

Meanwhile, the sands of time were running out for peace . . .

The Sunday Post 30th April 1939

The Sunday Post 7th May 1939

The Sunday Post 15th October 1939

Jings! The war hasn't even started yet
but Wullie's still managed to get into a skirmish!

The Sunday Post 21st May 1939

The Sunday Post 22nd October 1939

THE BROONS AND OOR WULLIE AT WAR 1939-1945

No fancy colas or fizzy pops here — sugarelly water was what young
folk craved in 1939.

The Sunday Post 28th May 1939

The Sunday Post 29th October 1939

The Sunday Post 5th November 1939

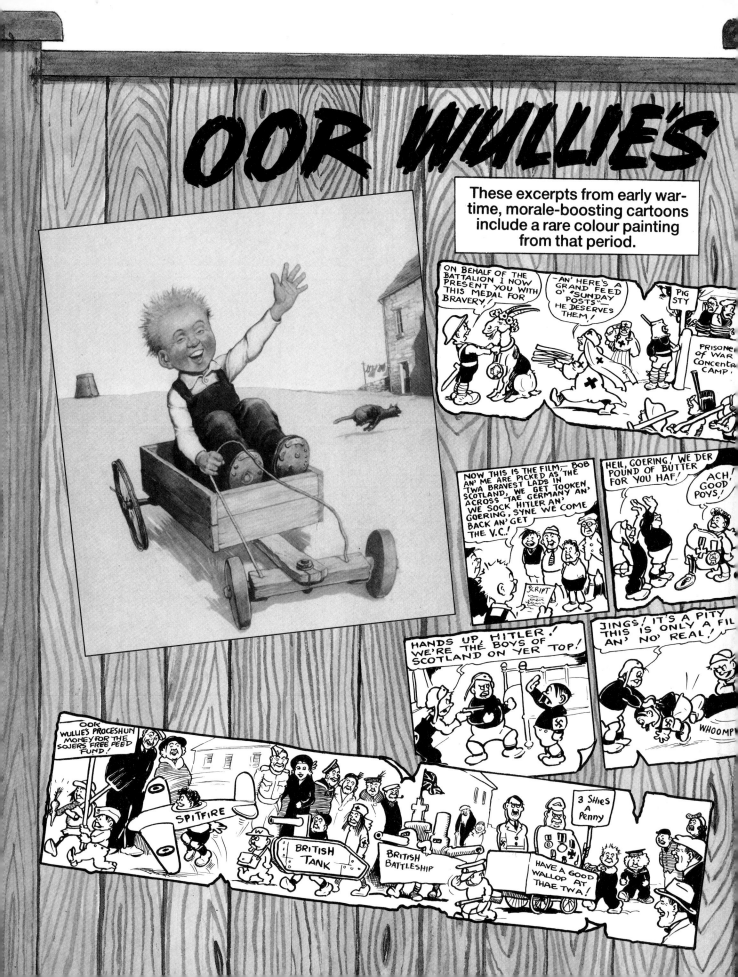

Even at the beginning of the war, efforts were being made to recycle and conserve resources. Everything was kept and used again and again. This became even more important after thousands lost everything during air-raids.

In the next few years, war-time paper shortages would result in the Dandy and Beano comics being published fortnightly instead of weekly and the size of The Sunday Post Fun Section being reduced. This also led to no Broons or Oor Wullie books being published between 1943 and 1947.

The Sunday Post 8th October 1939

THE BROONS AND OOR WULLIE AT WAR 1939-1945

The Sunday Post 19th November 1939

The Sunday Post 10th December 1939

The Sunday Post 24th December 1939

It seems that Maggie and Daphne had joined the Volunteer Aid Detachment (V.A.D.) whose job ranged from ambulance driving to performing blood transfusion.

The Sunday Post 17th December 1939

OOR WULLIE

Wha keeps his mother in a steer?
Wha nearly drives his father queer?
Wha throws the whole town oot o' gear?
  — Oor Wullie!
Wha has the teacher on a string?
Wha keeps the bobby wondering?
Wha pets his feet in everything?
  — Oor Wullie!

Wha is't, as soon's the day's begun,
Is thinking how we'll hae some fun,
And starts whene'er his breakfast's done?
  — Oor Wullie!
Wha ilka day has some ploy new,
And shares them a' wi me and you?
Wha dreams o' jokin' a' nicht through?
  — Oor Wullie!

Wha sits upon his wee zinc pail
And thinks oot schemes that canna fail?
— It puzzles me he's no in jail —
  — Oor Wullie!
Wha is't, whate'er the complication,
On each and every occasion
Has aye some handy explanation?
  — Oor Wullie!

Wha is't that in his dungarees
Sits thinking oot some brand-new wheeze
That sets fowk shaking at the knees?
  — Oor Wullie!
Wha is't, despite oor toil and trouble,
Wi' lauchin' gars us bend near double,
And maks us fair wi' pleasure bubble?
  — Oor Wullie!

Adapted from the Oor Wullie Annual 1940

1940

The nervous waiting for the all-clear siren during air-raids, listening to the wireless for every scrap of news about the war... with the fall of France and much of Western Europe to the Axis powers, Dunkirk and the Blitz, 1940 was a dark year in which Britain took a pounding. Even with the basics like bread, butter and bacon rationed, though, the UK was battered but not beaten. Taking a pop at Hitler and his cronies at every opportunity and making light of the situation was the order of the day. As the warden shown here is demonstrating, everything stops for tea!

The Sunday Post 28th January 1940

The Sunday Post 21st January 1940

This story shows Wullie being served up with school discipline of yesteryear — using one of Lochgelly's more notorious exports.

The Sunday Post 18th February 1940

The Sunday Post 24th March 1940

The Sunday Post 28th April 1940

The Sunday Post 21st April 1940

The Sunday Post 5th May 1940

The Sunday Post 12th May 1940

"A shillin' an' the tuppence" ... that's about six pence in today's money! That said, it would have bought you a Dandy AND a Beano in 1940 with change to spare!

The Sunday Post 22nd September 1940

Help! Paw and Granpaw Broon just aren't capable of looking after the kids on their own. But then, they just weren't used to doing 'women's work'. This story shows just one of the attitudes that wouldn't be featured these days!

This strip also illustrates well the type of games Scottish children were playing in 1940. The bombing and capturing of Nazi Germans was more than just make-believe. Everyone lived with daily stories of air-raids and this was brought even closer to home with the massive bombing of Clydebank in March 1941.

The Sunday Post 1st December 1940

The Sunday Post 8th December 1940

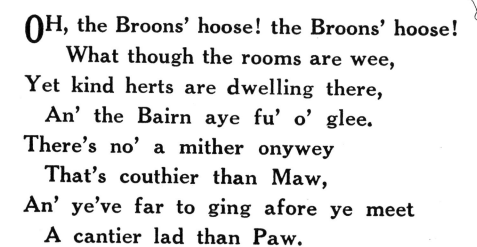

THE BROONS' HOOSE

OH, the Broons' hoose! the Broons' hoose!
　　What though the rooms are wee,
Yet kind herts are dwelling there,
　　An' the Bairn aye fu' o' glee.
There's no' a mither onywey
　　That's couthier than Maw,
An' ye've far to ging afore ye meet
　　A cantier lad than Paw.

There's Maggie, now ye can't deny
　　A treat she is tae see;
An' Daphne, if she's no' sae fair,
　　Is dear tae you an' me.
There's Hen and Joe, as fine a pair
　　O' lads as you could meet;
An Horace, busy wi' his books,
　　A' brains frae head tae feet.

Grandpaw's at ae end o' the line;
　　The twins are at the ither.
There's sure to be some fun aboot
　　When thae three get thegither.
And so at Glebe Street, Number Ten,
　　Ye're welcome, ane and a',
Tae pey a visit tae the Broons
　　An' laugh yer cares awa'.

Adapted from The Broons Annual 1941

1941

With German U-Boats sinking hundreds of thousands of tons of British shipping every month in the Battle of the Atlantic, extra pressure fell on the shipyards to refit old warships and build new ones. All records were smashed – 480 ships were built in the year to 1941.

Despite the air-raids on Clydeside, work carried on, and the Sunday Post of March 16th reported that "...The Government wants 50,000 more men for the shipyards..." and that any civilian over 20 who had recently worked in shipbuilding would be "called up".

Who knows, they could have found themselves working beside Paw Broon in the yards.

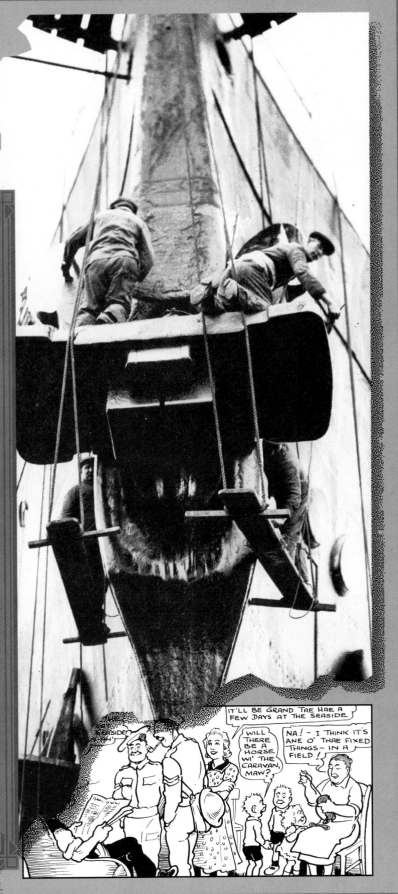

THE BROONS AND OOR WULLIE AT WAR 1939-1945

During the war years, everyone was encouraged to do their bit. Farmers and landowners were asked to turn over more of their land for food production and 'Dig For Victory'. Women worked hard on farms, digging, ploughing — even milking cows — to help with this.

This Broons strip illustrates one of the other things civilians were encouraged to do — learn first aid. If this story was to be believed, however, the results weren't quite what was expected!

The Sunday Post 19th January 1941

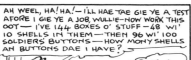

LISTEN TAE THIS MAW— IT SAYS HERE THAT FOLKS IN LESS IMPORTANT JOBS SHOULD JINE THE ARMY OR GANG IN TAE MUNITIONS!
THAT'S A BRAW IDEA! I'M JUIST WASTIN' MA TIME AT SCHULE!

TAE THINK I COULD BE HELPIN' IN THE WAR AN' A' THE TIME I'M JUIST DAEIN' LESSONS— WHIT'S THE USE O' HISTORY, GEOGRAPHY AN' SUMS— HUH!

JINGS! I MICHT EVEN GET MA NAME IN THE PAPERS— "THE BOY HERO!"
OOR WULLIE, THE BOY HERO, WORKS 28 HOURS A DAY AT HIS MACHINE!
OOR WULLIE MAKING SHELLS

FOUNDRY
HULLO, MR GRAY! I'M FED UP WI' ARITHMETIC AT SCHOOL, I WANT TAE MAK' MUNITIONS!
YE'RE FAR TOO WEE!

AH WEEL, HA! HA!— I'LL HAE TAE GIE YE A TEST AFORE I GIE YE A JOB, WULLIE—NOW WORK THIS OOT— I'VE 144 BOXES O' STUFF—48 WI' 10 SHELLS IN THEM—THEN 96 WI' 100 SOLDIERS BUTTONS—HOW MONY SHELLS AN BUTTONS DAE I HAVE?
7-6-56-8 —ER!

OCH AWA'— THAT'S SUMS! WE GET THAT AT THE SCHULE— I DINNA THINK I'D LIKE TAE WORK IN YER FOONDRY EFTER A'!
HA! HA! HA!

I WANT TAE JINE THE ARMY AS A DRUMMER BOY—I'M FED UP WI' SCHULE!
ARMY RECRUITING OFFICE
MICHTY ME!

AH WEEL, LADDIE, ANSWER THESE QUESTIONS— WHEN DID THE CRIMEAN WAR START AND FINISH? WHO WON THE BATTLE OF WATERLOO? WHO—
HE! HE! HE!
CRIMEAN WAR WIS—OH—ABOUT A HUNDER' YEAR AGO AN' I THINK NELSON WON THE BATTLE O' WATERLOO OR MEBBE IT WIS CROMWELL!

ACH TAE POT! THAT'S HISTORY— I'M FED UP WI' THAT AT THE SCHULE— OCH— I'LL NO' BOTHER JININ' THE ARMY!

HALF AN HOUR LATER
HULLO WULLIE!
JINGS! THERE'S RAB HAME FRAE THE SEA!

SAY, RAB, DINNA TELL MAW BUT I'M WANTIN' AWA' TAE THE SEA— I'M SICK O' DAEIN' SUMS AN' HISTORY AN' SPELLIN'!
OH? THAT'S THE STUFF! I'LL START YE AS SHIP'S CLERK, GET A PAPER AN' PENCIL!

NOW I WANT YE TAE WRITE DOON THE LIST O' CARGO. SIXTY TONS O' PHOSPHATES, 2000 BALES O' RAW JUTE, 100 TONS O' MANGANESE, 200 CRATES O'—
?

ACH! IT'S JUIST LIKE BEIN' AT A SPELLIN' LESSON!
cargo
60 tons fosfites
2000 bails raw joot
100 tons mag mangiknees

AW!—THERE'S AN R.A.F. OFFICER. I COULD ASK HIM IF I COULD GET INTAE THE AIR FORCE—BUT I BET THAT'S JUIST LIKE SCHULE TAE!

PLEASE, SIR, IS THE R.A.F. LIKE THE SCHULE?

SCOTLAND
NOW YOU MUST KNOW WHERE ALL THE CHIEF TOWNS, RIVERS, MOUNTAINS, HEADLANDS AND FIRTHS AND BAYS ARE SITUATED!

THANKS VERY MUCH, SIR— THAT'S A' I WANT TAE KEN!

JINGS! I'VE JUIST MINDED—THIS IS FRIDAY—THE DAY TEACHER LETS US READ "THE DANDY" A' LAST HOUR!

IN SCHOOL
OCH!, SCHULES NO' SAE BAD!
DANDY

AYE, I'LL JUIST STAY AT THE SCHOOL, I'LL NO BOTHER THE NOO ABOOT HAEIN' MA NAME IN THE PAPERS!

AW JINGS — EIGHT O'CLOCK AGAIN!

YAWN

THERE WIS SOMETHING I HAD TAE MIND ABOOT THE SCHULE TO-DAY. NOO WHIT WIS IT? — POETRY? OR SUMS? — OR WASH MA FACE?

I'LL BETTER LEARN MA POETRY ANY WAY — "THE BOY STOOD ON THE BURNING DECK, WHENCE ALL BUT HE HAD FLED — " M-M — M-M — M-M! — OCH! I KEN THAT!

IT'S TIME YE WERE UP, WULLIE! — "NOW, GEOGRAPHY — NEW YORK IS THE LARGEST AMERICAN CITY — MOUNT EVEREST IS 29,000 FT. HIGH" — OCH I KEN A' THAT TAE!

MEBBE IT WIS TAE HAE MA NECK WASHED — I'LL DAE THAT.

1 MINUTE LATER — THAT'S MA NECK WASHED — WEEL, IT'S A KINDA WASHED!

I'LL BRUSH MA HAIR NICE TAE! JINGS! I WISH I COULD MIND WHIT IT WIS I FORGOT!

MEBBE IT WIS TAE CLEAN MA BOOTS!

YE'LL NEED TAE LOOK SHARP, WULLIE, IT'S HALF PAST EIGHT!

AYE - BUT I'M TRYIN' TAE MIND SOMETHIN' MA!

I'LL EAT MA ROLL ON THE ROAD TAE THE SCHULE, MA.

THIS IS TERRIBLE I CANNA MIND WHIT IT WIS I HAD TAE REMEMBER!

HEY, WULLIE —
DINNA BOTHER ME IN THE NOO! — I'M BUSY REMEMBERING!

HA! HA! HA!!
I'LL REPEAT MA HISTORY AGAIN — JULIUS CAESAR - 1066, ROBERT BRUCE - ER - ABOOT 1745 OR WIS IT 1815, ACH! - TAE POT!
9 TIMES 1 ARE 9,
9 TIMES 2 ARE 16,
9 TIMES 3 ARE 28,
2 PINTS 1 QUART,
4 QUARTS 1 TON,
16 TONS EQUAL
1 ACRE!

I KEN, I'LL SHARPEN A' MA PENCILS — MEBBE THAT WIS IT!

— UNLESS IT WIS TAE PICK FLOWERS FOR THE TEACHER.

NOW I'M A' THE ROAD! I HAVENA' FORGOTTEN A THING NOO, I'M SURE!

AW JINGS! I MIND NOO! IT'S A HOLIDAY THE DAY-THE SCHULE'S SHUT TAE BE PENTED !!
SCHOOL!

WHOOPEE!

— AN' TAE THINK I WASHED MA NECK FOR NOTHING!
WASHED!

The Sunday Post 23rd February 1941

The Sunday Post 30th March 1941

THE BROONS AND OOR WULLIE AT WAR 1939-1945

The Sunday Post 4th May 1941

The Sunday Post 20th April 1941

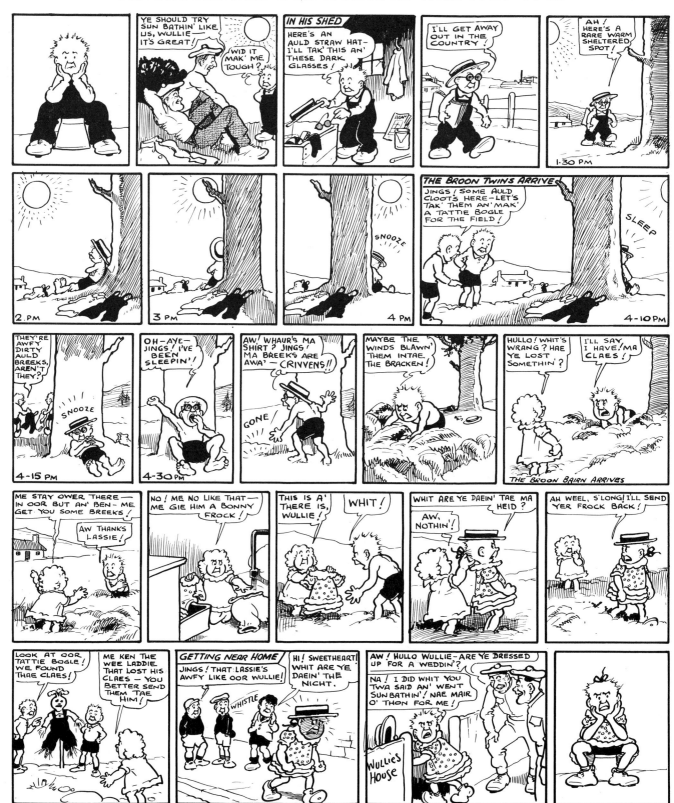

It looks like no one had ever heard of sun-block cream in those days.

The Sunday Post 6th July 1941

The Sunday Post 2nd November 1941

The Sunday Post 2nd November 1941

The Sunday Post 23rd November 1941

The Sunday Post 7th December 1941

The Sunday Post 28th December 1941

THE SUNDAY PO...

The Sunday Post

Morning Special

PRINTED AND PUBLISHED IN GLASGOW EVERY SUNDAY MORNING

NO. 1775. [REGISTERED AT THE GENERAL POST OFFICE AS A NEWSPAPER] SUNDAY, SEPTEMBER 3, 1939. RADIO—PAGE 3 PRICE TWOPENCE.

Here are some of the headlines that appeared during 1939-1942.

GERMAN FORCES MUST WITHDRAW

R.A.F. BOMB GERMAN TROOPS

RESCUE ARMADA KEEPS IT UP

BERLIN BOMBED FOR FIRST TIME IN TWO WARS

MORE NAZI BOMBERS DOWN

R.A.F.'s ALL-DAY RAIDS ON GUERNSEY

R.A.F. ATTACK NAZI NAVAL BASES

MIDNIGHT RAID ON LONDON AREA

LONDON WOMEN SHOPPERS MACHINE-GUNNED

MILE OF FIRES RAGE IN BERLIN

8th ARMY'S MASSIVE ATTACK

OOR WULLIE, YOUR WULLIE, A'BODY'S WULLIE

1942

This year brought fresh hope for the people of Britain; the Americans had joined the war effort after the attack on Pearl Harbour the previous December; victory at El Alamein in October put Rommel's Afrika Korps on the run in North Africa, and the entire German Sixth Army was swallowed up in the siege at Stalingrad.

On the Home Front, putting up black-out shutters and counting the clothing coupons had become a way of life. Air Raid Precautions Wardens (ARPs) took to using boy messengers to carry out errands, as shown here, though not without problems: the Sunday Post of February 22nd noted that wardens in Cowdenbeath had been supplied with overalls so over-sized that "the trousers extended to the neck and the bodies reached to the knees".

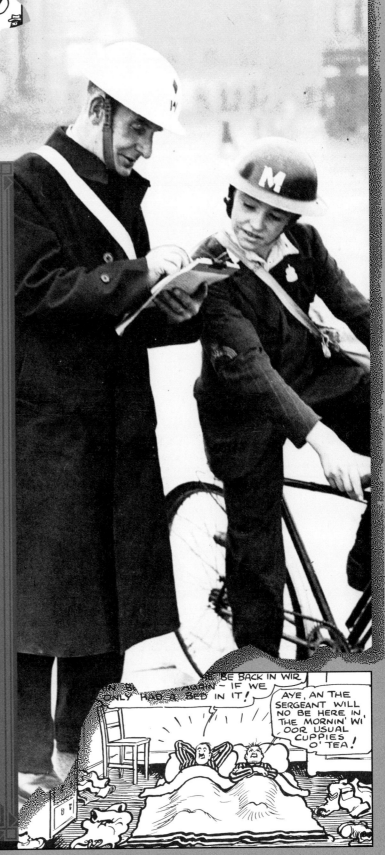

WHIT LOVELY DEEP SNOW! I WISH I HAD A SLEDGE. JINGS — THERE'S AN AULD PRAM WI'OOT WHEELS AT THE BACK O' MA SHED!

MY! THIS IS THE VERY THING — IF I HAD A DOG TAE PULL THE SLEDGE I COULD BE A REAL NORTH POLE EXPLORER!

Wullie's Shed.

I KEN — I'LL START A NORTH POLE EXHIBITION- EXPI-EXPEDITION — AN' GET FAT BOB AN' THEM TAE COME — I'LL PIT THIS AXE AN' COMPASS AN' FIREWID AN' THINGS IN MA SLED — THEN I'LL GET THE LEN' O' TAM HENDERSON'S DOG!

HI, BOYS! I'M AWA' TAE THE NORTH POLE — ARE YE COMIN'?

NA! NA! IT'S OWER NEAR DINNER TIME TAE GANG TAE THE NORTH POLE!

NO' FOR ME — WE'D BE OWER LATE GETTIN' BACK THE NICHT!

OCH! YE'RE A COUPLE O' SAFTIES — FEARDIE GOATS — I'LL GANG A' BY MASEL' — I'M TOUGH — AN' I'VE GOT A WEE COMPASS AN' I'LL JUST KEEP GAUN NORTH A' THE TIME!

OCH! YOU'LL NO GET TAE THE NORTH POLE THE DAY — IT'S OWER FAR!

HA! HA! HA!

NOO I'VE TAE CROSS THIS BURN TAE KEEP GOIN' NORTH MA COMPASS IS POINTIN' THIS WAY!

MY! THIS IS DEEP SNOW! AH — BUT IT'S NOTHIN' TAE WHIT EXPLORERS GET!

FURTHER SOUTH

HEY BOB, HAE YE SEEN WULLIE?

AYE! HE WENT AWA' TAE THE NORTH POLE ABOOT AN HOUR SYNE!

THE NORTH POLE !! WHICH WAY DID HE GO?

HE SAID HE WIS FOLLOWIN' HIS COMPASS DUE NORTH!

COME ON, MA — WE'LL HEAD NORTH AN' LOOK FOR HIM!

WE'LL HELP YE! YE KEN HE MICHT MISS HIS WAY AN' GANG RICHT PAST THE NORTH POLE!

THERE IT IS!

JINGS! I'VE FOUND IT!

I'LL NEED TAE TAK' IT BACK WI' ME OR MA PALS WILL NOT BELIEVE ME!

WIFIE WITH WASHING

JINGS! HERE'S WULLIE NOO! HE'S BROCHT THE NORTH POLE BACK WI' HIM!

HI, WULLIE! HOO DAE YE KEN IT'S THE NORTH POLE!

WEEL — MA COMPASS POINTED STRAIGHT AT IT!

YE YOUNG SCAMP! YE'LL HAE TAE PAY FOR THIS — CUTTIN' DOON MA CLOTHES POLE AN' ME WANTIN' TAE HANG OOT MA WASHIN' — !!

HA! HA! HA! IT'S THE WIFIE'S GREENIE POLE YE TOOK!

LOOK MISSUS — HERE'S HAUF A CROWN — BUY YERSEL' ANITHER POLE!

The Sunday Post 12th April 1942

The Sunday Post 19th April 1942

Today's editorial team would steer clear
of this reckless fire-raising!

The Sunday Post 10th May 1942

Wullie wouldn't get away with this kind of baby-sitting today!

The Sunday Post 31st May 1942

The Sunday Post 12th July 1942

The Sunday Post 16th August 1942

The Sunday Post 27th September 1942

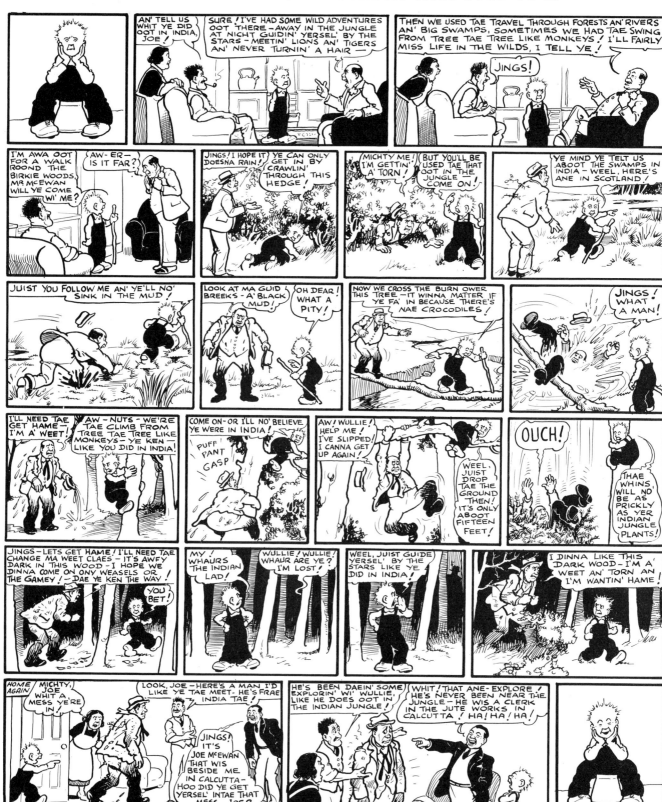

The Sunday Post 25th October 1942

The Sunday Post 29th November 1942

The Sunday Post 15th November 1942

The Sunday Post 27th December 1942

AT THE BARBER'S

Adapted from 'Oor Wullie' April 16th, 1944, these sketches show how the use of simple black and white artwork with strong lines bring the characters to life. Wullie still gets up to all sorts in The Sunday Post every week and is as popular as ever.

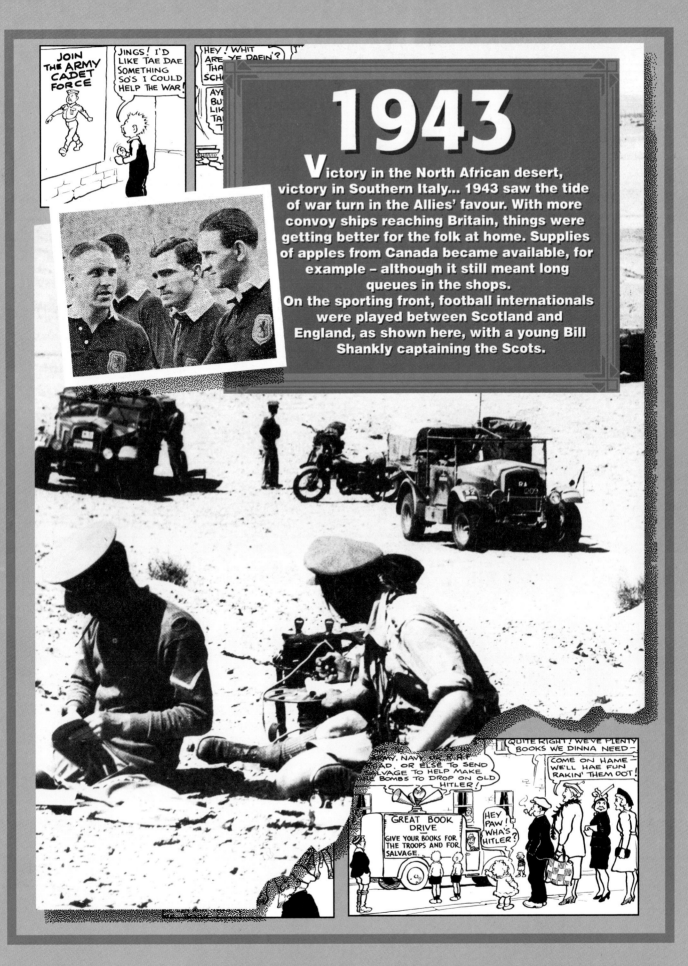

1943

Victory in the North African desert, victory in Southern Italy... 1943 saw the tide of war turn in the Allies' favour. With more convoy ships reaching Britain, things were getting better for the folk at home. Supplies of apples from Canada became available, for example – although it still meant long queues in the shops.
On the sporting front, football internationals were played between Scotland and England, as shown here, with a young Bill Shankly captaining the Scots.

The Sunday Post 28th February 1943

The Sunday Post 3rd January 1943

The Sunday Post 21st March 1943

The Sunday Post 10th January 1943

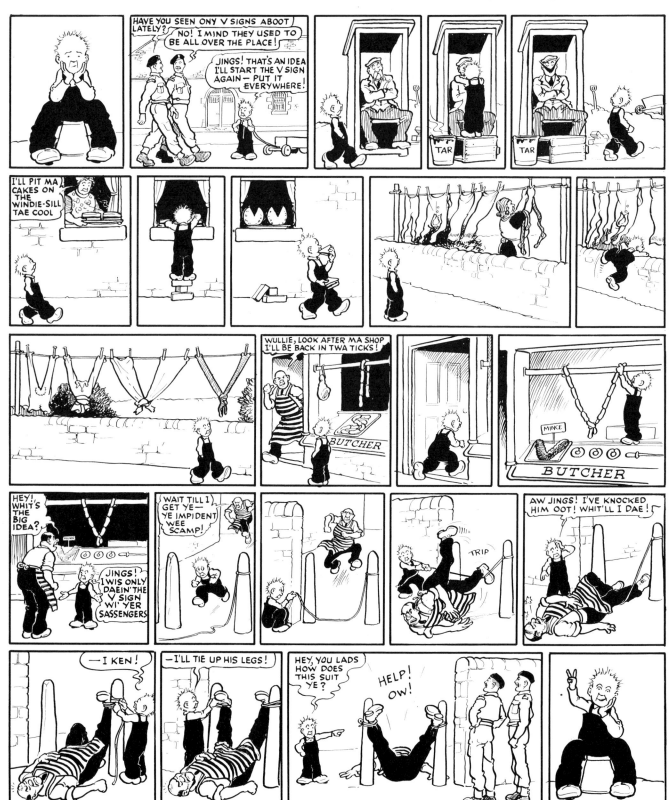

Pages from this period herald a noticeable shift in the artist's style.

The Sunday Post 31st January 1943

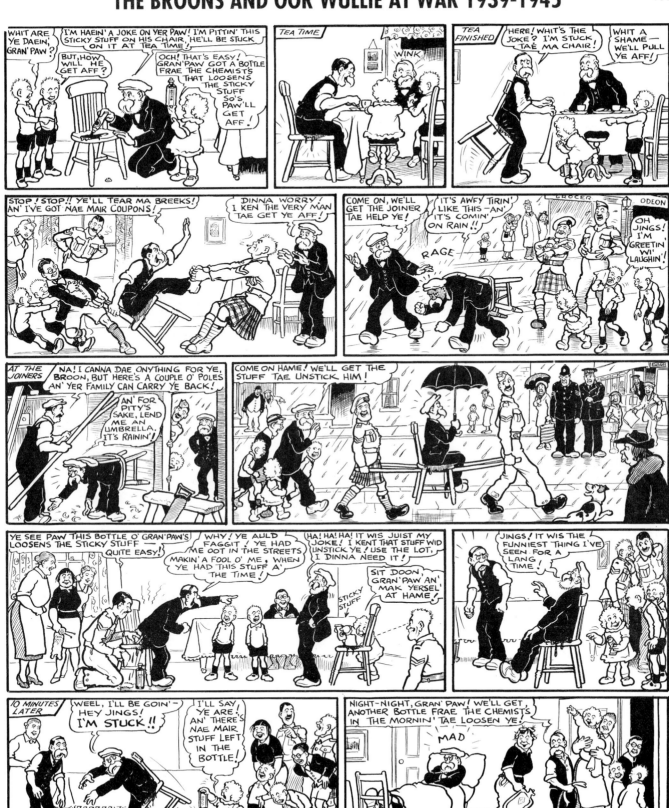

The Sunday Post 7th February 1943

The Supermarine Spitfire — symbol of Britain's defiance in the Battle of Britain — would have been a very sought-after model kit during the war.

The Sunday Post 7th November 1943

The Sunday Post 14th February 1943

The Sunday Post 5th December 1943

The Sunday Post 28th February 1943

The Sunday Post 12th December 1943

The Sunday Post 19th December 1943

The Sunday Post 5th September 1943

DOMESTIC BLISS

Life at No. 10 Glebe Street is never quiet. These sketches show the instantly recognisable characters of 'The Broons', still much loved after more than 60 years.

Adapted from 'The Broons' May 21st, 1944

YE'RE IN THE HOME GUARD NOW,
—SO, LEFT TURN, RICHT TURN,
RICHT WHEEL, ABOOT TURN—
HALT!—JINGS! THIS IS GREAT!

I'VE STARTE[D]
GUARD AN[D]
OFFICERS FO[R]
A PARADE AT
THE TROO[P]

1944

June 6th: D-Day! Operation Overlord, the Allied invasion of Normandy swung into action with one of the largest troop operations of all time. At last there was real optimism at home – the war was no longer merely being fought, it was being won! Sunday Post readers were encouraged to submit cartoons for Pinhead Percy, as shown below. Despite clothing shortages and rationing, some of our lads serving abroad had other priorities. One seaman, whose letter was published, wrote: "Thank ye... for the Broons and Oor Wullie. Although it's a month or twa since we last saw them, a'body goes daft ower them".

PERCY ON THE BEACHES !

This week's adventure of Pinhead Percy comes from Denis Healy, jun., Sandyhills, Glasgow, E.2.

The Sunday Post 6th February 1944

THE BROONS AND OOR WULLIE AT WAR 1939-1945

The Sunday Post 13th February 1944

The Sunday Post 20th February 1944

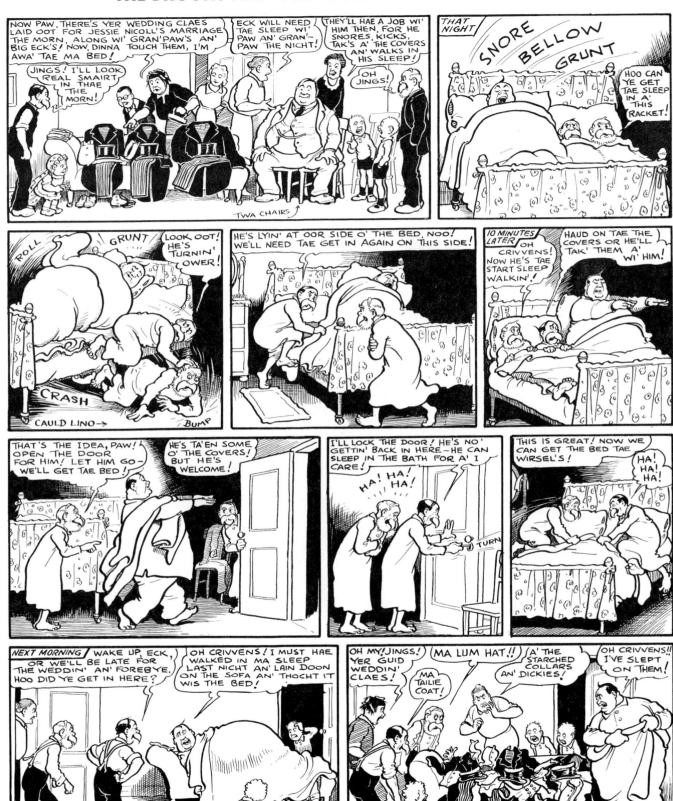

The Sunday Post 26th March 1944

The Sunday Post 9th July 1944

The Sunday Post 9th July 1944

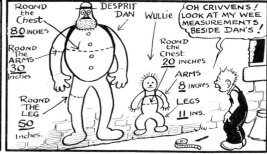

The Sunday Post 30th July 1944

THE BROONS AND OOR WULLIE AT WAR 1939-1945

123

The Sunday Post 6th August 1944

The Sunday Post 6th August 1944

The Sunday Post 8th October 1944

The Sunday Post 17th December 1944

THE SUNDAY POST. AUGUST 1, 1943.

The Sunday Post

Morning Special

PRINTED AND PUBLISHED IN GLASGOW EVERY SUNDAY MORNING.

NO. 1979. [REGISTERED AT THE GENERAL POST OFFICE AS A NEWSPAPER.] SUNDAY, AUGUST 1, 1943. RADIO—PAGE 10 PRICE TWOPENCE.

These headlines appeared during the years 1943-1945.

EISENHOWER'S ULTIMATUM TO ITALY

Great Day For Red Army
THREE IMPORTANT TOWNS TAKEN BY STORM

Rome Cries "Peace" As Monty's Men Press On

Half Of Hitler Line Smashed

120 Miles From German Border
Our Troops Streaming Over The Seine
NO ESCAPE NOW FOR 45,000 NAZIS

35 MILES TO ANZIO

Monty's Men Reach Th Rhine

RED ARMY IN BERLIN

GERMANY'S UNCONDITIONAL SURRENDER REPORTED

All Over Bar The Signing
—U.S. VIEW
Allied Marines Waiting To Land In Japan

JAPANESE SIGNED THIS MORNING
SURRENDER CEREMONY ON BOARD THE MISSOURI

1945

VE Day, (Victory in Europe Day) on May 8th was declared a national holiday. Nelson's Column in Trafalgar Square, the focus for some of the biggest crowds, was specially floodlit, as was Westminster Abbey and the Houses of Parliament. King George VI and the Queen later visited Edinburgh as part of the celebrations.

Not only did VE Day signal the end of the war in Europe – it meant the end for the dreaded black-out too! Within a week all black-out orders had been revoked, with the last places to go being Orkney and Shetland.

The Sunday Post 21st January 1945

The Sunday Post 28th January 1945

The Sunday Post 4th March 1945

The Sunday Post 11th February 1945

The Sunday Post 18th March 1945

THE BROONS AND OOR WULLIE AT WAR 1939-1945

The Sunday Post 11th November 1945

OOR WULLIE

Hurray! Let's celebrate! After six long years, Victory in Europe Day was declared on May 8th, 1945. Wullie and millions of others throughout the country were overjoyed. Here we see that Wullie couldn't even be annoyed with his life-long 'enemies' PC Murdoch and the dreaded Heidmaster!

The Sunday Post 2nd December 1945

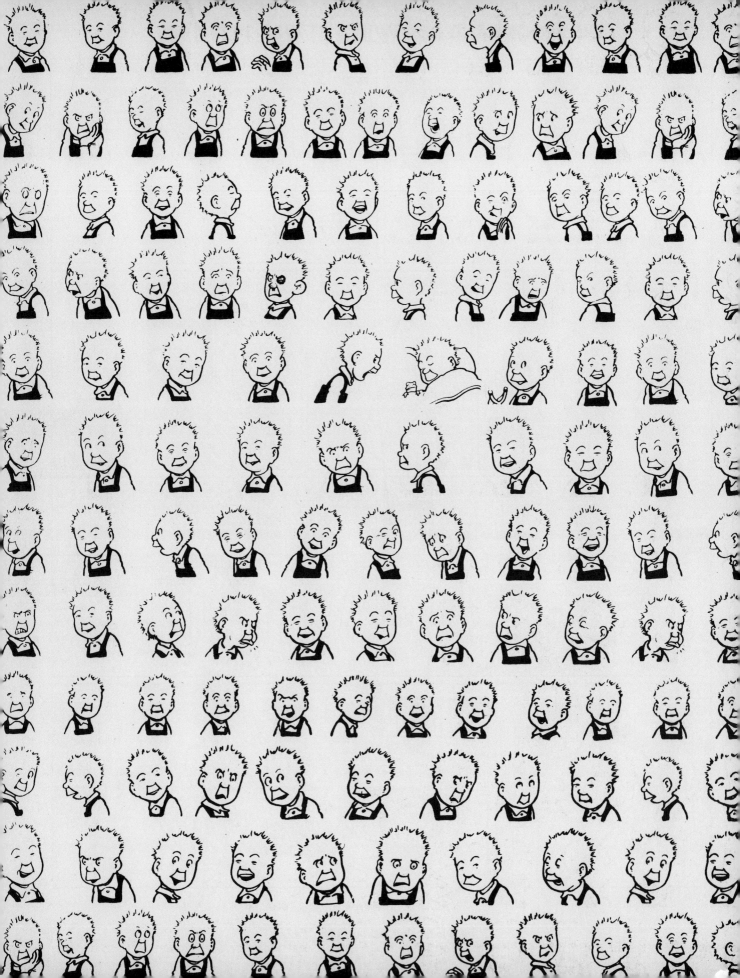